Super
What-a-Mess

Frank Muir
Illustrated by Joseph Wright

Copyright © 1980, 1984 by Frank Muir
Illustrations Copyright © 1980 by Joseph Wright
Published by Price/Stern/Sloan Publishers, Inc.
410 North La Cienega Boulevard, Los Angeles, California 90048

ISBN: 0-8431-1041-4

PRICE/STERN/SLOAN
Publishers, Inc., Los Angeles
1984

What-a-Mess was enjoying a snooze.
It was the seventeenth snooze of the thirty or so he usually
enjoyed on a hot summer's day and he was having it in his
new Top-Secret Hiding-Place—a small garbage can behind the old barn

The garbage can was so small and What-a-Mess was so fat a puppy
that he stuck out of the top, but he balanced the
lid on his head and reckoned he was as good as invisible.
And he was dreaming his favorite dream . . .

Crowds in the street stared up at the tiny dot racing across the sky at incredible speed.

"Is it a fat, scruffy spaceship?"

"Is it a bionic doormat?"

"No. It's SUPER WHAT-A-MESS!!!!"

4

When the young girl of the house sat watching television,
she allowed What-a-Mess to lie on the floor and watch with her.
As long as he did not fidget too much or get sick with
excitement (which he did once).
The one program which he really loved was "Superman" . . .

POOOOOOW!
It was Super What-a-Mess to the rescue at the speed of sound.
WHAAAAAM!
Super What-a-Mess's paw went straight to the jaw of the Evil
Menace who was threatening the World and knocked him out cold.
The fight was over.
Another triumph for . . . . . . SUPER WHAT-A-MESS!!!

What-a-Mess woke happily from his dream and
trotted back to the house.

It was the last time he was to be happy for weeks.
His troubles started when he heard his mother calling him.
Eager not to keep her waiting, he tried to dive at top speed
through the cat-door. There was a tremendous CLANG!,
his head felt as though it had been hit with a sledgehammer
and he reeled back, eyes watering.
He had forgotten he was still wearing the garbage can lid.

The people in the house grabbed him with cries of
"Look at him! What a mess!
And little Poppet arriving any moment!"
Then they scraped his coat with a painful steel comb and tied
a pink bow round his neck. He felt awful.

Worse was yet to come.
"Little Poppet" usually went to the kennel when her
house was shut for the holidays; but this year,
she was coming to stay with What-a-Mess and his mother.

"She has been nicely brought up," said his mother firmly,
"so you must be on your best behavior.
She's only here for a month and it will be nice to have a
little cousin to play with. You are not to stay indoors in this
lovely weather watching television. Take her out in the garden."
No television! No Superman! For a MONTH!

Poppet turned out to be small, well-behaved and
neat as a pin. She wagged her tail and then sat up
and begged and everyone went "aaaaah."
When her name was spoken, she gave a happy little "yap!"
and rolled on her back to be tickled. What-a-Mess had
never disliked another living thing so much
in the whole of his short, fat, scruffy life.

But he did try to behave well.
He took Poppet on a tour of the garden.
Once out of sight of the house, she bit What-a-Mess most painfully in the leg and ran off into the shrubs.
He gave chase, got his coat hopelessly tangled in thorns, stepped in a wasps' nest and was thoroughly chewed out when he got back to the house. Poppet returned neat and clean and was cuddled.

Still What-a-Mess tried.
He let her join him in his traditional sport of chasing the cat-next-door. Poppet, whose twinkling legs carried her at an unbelievable speed, caught the cat and nipped him hard. Several times. Mostly on the tail, which was his best feature.

When the lady-next-door saw the damaged tail, she hit What-a-Mess a painful blow on the nose with a folded copy of *The Times*. Poppet rolled over and she tickled Poppet's tummy.

"Now listen, Poppet," said What-a-Mess, a few dreadful days later.
"Dogs are meant to chase cats. It's all part of Nature.
But they are not supposed to *catch* them!"

"Don't you tell me what I'm supposed to do!" yapped Poppet.
"Do you think I wanted to come to this boring dump for my holiday?
I hate boring grass and boring gardens and boring Afghan puppies.
I like the boarding kennel. I used to sleep all day on
nice sawdust and bark all night to keep the other dogs awake.
That's what I call fun! Now that I've been dragged here,
I'm going to make you suffer for it!"

With which she jumped up and pushed over a pedestal on which
was poised a vase of flowers. People rushed in to find out
what the noise was about. Poppet yapped furiously at What-a-Mess,
then sat up and begged. She was given a chocolate cookie;
What-a-Mess was sent to bed without supper.

The next morning, What-a-Mess and the cat-next-door held a
council-of-war.
They were in What-a-Mess's Second-Best Secret Hiding-Place,
a rusty, discarded baby carriage.
"Funny, really, when you come to think about it," said the cat.
"You and me, arch-enemies, sworn to perpetual warfare until
one of us doth perish, and here we are sitting together in a baby buggy."

"Never mind that," said What-a-Mess. "How do we rid ourselves
of the Evil Menace?"
They sat in thought for a while.
"It's hopeless," said the cat. "She runs faster than we can.
She bites harder. It would take more than a scruffy
hound to beat *her* in a battle. It would take *super* hound."

Lights flashed in What-a-Mess's brain. A super hound?
SUPER WHAT-A-MESS! POOOOW! WHAAAAM!
"That's it!" cried What-a-Mess. "Superman is just a meek little man until he changes in the telephone booth. All I need is a scarlet cloak and a huge 'S' on my chest and I will have incredible super-power! Quick, find out where the Evil Menace is and I'll super myself."
He leaped out of the baby carriage and raced for the house.

The red cloak was easy to find; the daughter of the house
was going to a party that evening and her long, red dress had just
come back from the cleaners. What-a-Mess took the wire hanger
in his teeth and raced back across the garden, trailing the dress
behind him. The big 'S' was more difficult.
Eventually, he found a huge iron 'S' on the side of the barn,
the sort used to keep walls from bulging and falling down.
Luckily, it was loose and What-a-Mess managed to turn it round
and round until it fell off.

As there was no telephone booth in the garden, What-a-Mess
decided that changing in his little garbage can would be
just as effective. It was an awkward squeeze and someone had poured
in a gallon of old motor oil since he had last used it;
but he managed at last and emerged a splendid figure,
cloaked in scarlet with the huge iron 'S' on his chest and—
because of the oil—little black bootees.

The cat returned to report that Poppet was asleep
in a deckchair round the other side of the house.

What-a-Mess worked out his plan.

"I will climb onto the roof," he announced to the cat,
"then, launch myself into the sky at supersonic speed—VROOOOOOM!
A mile up, I will turn and hurtle down upon the Evil Menace—
PEEEEOOOOW!—and then—WOOOW! ZAPPP! SPLATTT!"

Climbing onto the roof was much harder than he had thought.
The iron 'S' kept banging against his chest, his feet
caught in the cloak, and he felt dizzy.
Helped by the cat, whose head he used as a stepping stone,
he clambered onto the water barrel, up the sloping side of the
tool shed and then onto the roof itself.
He had never felt so awful in his life.

"Don't look down!" shouted the cat.

What-a-Mess lay spreadeagled on the roof, clinging on miserably.
Eventually, he began to work his way along until he was above
Poppet's deckchair. It was then that he made his big mistake.
He tried to stand up.

His feet, slippery with black oil, slid in all directions
and he lost his hold. Slowly at first and then faster and faster
he slithered down towards the edge.

Below on a cushion, full of expensive canned food, dozed Poppet.
A muffled yelp of panic above her caused her to open one eye.
There, hurtling down on top of her was a terrifying monster,
with huge, red wings and a great 'S'-shaped iron nose . . .

Poppet gave one fearful "Yap!" and ran for it.
When last glimpsed, she had cleared the back fence and was
racing at about forty knots in the direction of the
Sunnyside Boarding Kennel for Dogs.

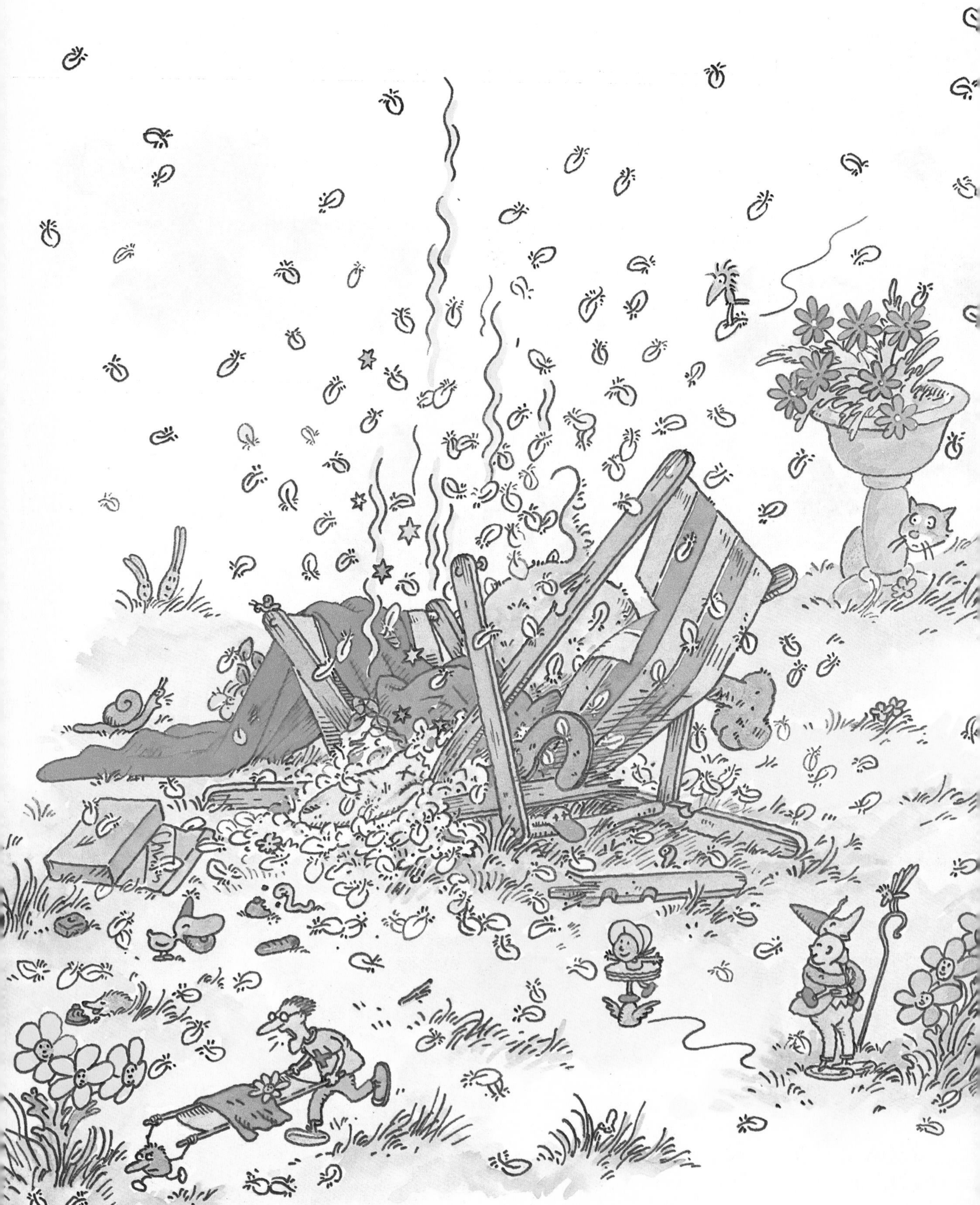

There was a great deal of shouting and rushing about, of course, but What-a-Mess hardly heard it.
The deckchair had broken his fall but he was completely winded.

The following morning, at television time, the girl of the
house dragged What-a-Mess in his basket to a nice place
in front of the set. He was having a snooze at the time.
"Thank you, What-a-Mess," she whispered, thinking, wrongly,
that he could not hear her.
"Thank you for ruining my red dress last night.
How did you guess that I didn't want to go to that party?
Oh, What-a-Mess, you are a SUPER hound!"

"Not any more!" thought What-a-Mess to himself. "And I don't, ever, want to be again!"
And rather than bother to watch television, he let himself sink from a snooze into a lovely, dreamless sleep.